For Bruno, Noah, Tibo & Gabriel

D1335918

Thank you to
Talia Yahya, Molly Freshwater & Halo Design

DAVID
THE DINOSAUR

by Adam Black

illustrated by
Màriam Ben-Arab

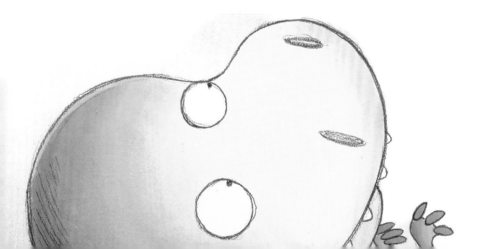

David the Dinosaur didn't like dogs,
He didn't like cats or horses or frogs.
He didn't like to tidy his box of toys,
But he really liked eating plump little boys.

Plump little boys tasted especially good.
He liked them for starters or even his pud.
He liked them on bread or even on toast,
He liked them for breakfast or for his Sunday roast.

He had once eaten a girl in the middle of the night.
He'd climbed through her window and given her a fright.

But her long blond hair had got stuck in his throat,
And he couldn't swallow the buttons on her pretty pink coat.

So it was boys for him from that moment on,
He loved the way they slipped over his tongue.
He liked them more than eating fruit and nuts
Which his *mum* made him eat – no 'ifs' and no 'buts'.

On Monday morning he climbed out of his cave,
He gave his mother and father a wave.
He walked down the hill and out of the wood,
and off he went in search of some food.

He hadn't eaten anything
since Friday lunch,
When he'd eaten a boy in
just one munch.

RUMBLE RUMBLE!!

But now his tummy was
starting to whine,
And he knew it was well
past his dinner time.

He swam over the river and crept towards town.
He walked on his toes so he made little sound.
He spotted some boys at play in the street,
He knew he was in for a feast and a treat.

He pounced on a boy and a big bite he did take,
But knew right away it was a massive mistake.

His mouth was in pain, his tongue was on fire,
His eyes were watering, he thought he'd expire.

Smoke started coming from the end of his nose.
He felt aches and pains in the tips of his toes.
His bones were hurting, his heart beating fast,
And deep down inside he knew this boy was his last.

He looked at the body of the boy on the ground,
And was immediately surprised by what he had found.
The head filled with pins, the hands filled with nails,
The dummy's arms and legs stuffed with porcupine tails.

The boys in the town weren't going to be beaten,
They'd seen too many friends being chased and then eaten.
They had planned and had schemed and had lain in wait,
And David the Dinosaur had taken the bait.

Deadly Dave had learnt a valuable lesson in life,
Stop snacking on boys... and get himself a wife.

She might cook him bowls of steam boiled fish,
There was very little danger in this kind of dish.

It was the end of the day, the beginning of night,
And David the Dinosaur looked an awful sight.
He slunk into his cave and went straight to bed,
Not even a bedtime story was read.

He woke the next day, both hungry and sore,
He went to the fridge and found veg that was raw.
He liked what he ate, and resolved from that day,
To never eat boys again, come what may.

THE END

Fun Stuff

Now that you've read the book, try and
see if you can answer these questions...